Lucky Christmas

Lucky Christmas

c. 2

BETSY DUFFEY

illustrated by Leslie Morrill

SIMON & SCHUSTER BOOKS FOR YOUNG READERS
Published by Simon & Schuster
New York London Toronto Sydney Tokyo Singapore

For Nick

SIMON & SCHUSTER BOOKS FOR YOUNG READERS
1230 Avenue of the Americas
New York, New York 10020
Text copyright © 1994 by Betsy Duffey
Illustrations copyright © 1994 by Leslie Morrill
All rights reserved including the right of
reproduction in whole or in part in any form.
SIMON & SCHUSTER BOOKS FOR YOUNG READERS
is a trademark of Simon & Schuster.
The text for this book is set in 14-point Primer
Manufactured in the United States of America

10 9 8 7 6 5 4 3 2 1

Library of Congress Cataloging-in-Publication Data
Duffey, Betsy.
  Lucky Christmas / by Betsy Duffey ; illustrated by Leslie Morrill.
    p. cm.
  Summary: When Great-Aunt Octavia's visit banishes his dog Lucky
from the house, George tries to get him reinstated in time for
Christmas.
  [1. Dogs—Fiction. 2. Great-aunts—Fiction. 3. Christmas—Fic-
tion.] I. Morrill, Leslie H., ill. II. Title.
PZ7.D876Ls 1994 [Fic]—dc20 93-41092 CIP AC
ISBN: 0-671-86425-4

Contents

Aunt Octopus

George was packing his things into a cardboard box. His baseball glove. His bat. His Nolan Ryan baseball card.

His mother's aunt, Aunt Octavia, was coming for Christmas. And she was staying in HIS room.

There were some good things about Aunt Octavia. He liked the way she looked—soft and wrinkled. He liked the way she smelled—like cinnamon. She always had time to play cards with him and she told the best stories. But there were other things about her that he did not like.

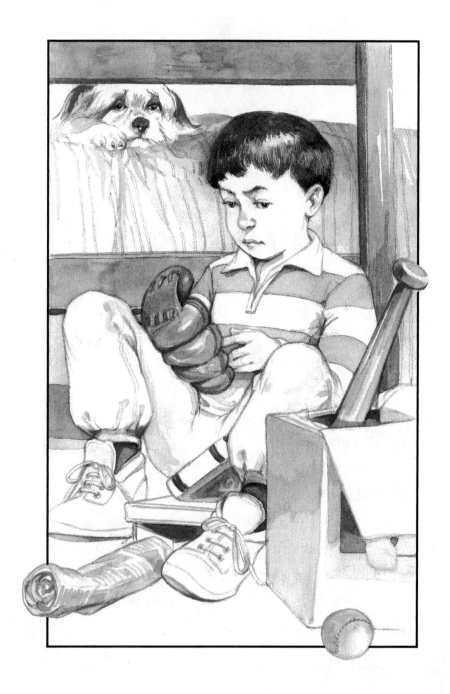

She always wrapped her arms around him and *squeezed* like an octopus. Aunt Octopus, George called her.

She would say, "How's my favorite nephew? Now give us a hug!"

She would smother him with octopus hugs. Then she would slime him with octopus kisses.

It was too gross to think about.

George packed his pinewood derby car and his space rock. He looked at the rest of the stuff on his shelf and sighed. The box was too small for everything.

He hoped Aunt Octopus wouldn't bother his things. "Tidy up," she called it. When she "tidied up," it meant getting rid of his stuff. Good stuff, too.

One time she threw out his bug zoo. It had taken him weeks to gather all the bugs. "Unsanitary," she said. Then in one flush they were gone.

He hoped Aunt Octavia wouldn't offer to cook. She always made casseroles. Mixtures of things with strange names. Gazpacho or parmigiana. One time he saw a fish eye in one. His mother said it was a black olive but he was never sure about it.

He hoped that she hadn't bought his Christmas present at a yard sale this year. One year she had given him a glow-in-the-dark painting of Elvis Presley on black velvet. Elvis stared at him from above the bed. His mother always put it out when Aunt Octopus came.

His aunt loved that painting. She always walked into his room and talked to it. She'd say, "Elvis, you hound dog!"

Most of all, he hoped that she would like Lucky. Last visit he had not had a dog. Lucky stared at him from the bottom of the bed.

Lucky's brown eyes watched George as he packed. George put Lucky's rubber newspaper in the box. Lucky whined.

Aunt Octopus didn't seem like the kind of person who would like dogs. George remembered the bug zoo. It didn't look good for

"You're not unsanitary, are you?" he
_ky. Lucky thumped his tail.
_cked up the box and walked to his
_edroom. His sleeping bag was al-
_ed out on the floor.
_eping here," he told Lucky.
_ped onto the sleeping bag. He
_nd rubbed his back.
_ber, Lucky, don't jump up on Aunt

Erf!

"And don't chew any of her things."
Erf!
"And don't bark at her."
Erf! Erf!
George reached over and picked up Lucky.

George buried his face in Lucky's back. "It's only for two days," he said. "Just be good for two days. Just until Christmas is over."

"George, is your room ready?" George's mother hurried in, carrying an armload of towels.

"Yes."

"Remember, George, be polite to your aunt."

"Okay."

"And don't bother her room."

"Okay!"

"And have nice manners at the table."

"Okay! Okay!"

Honk! Honk!

George and his mother looked out the window. A big black car was pulling into the driveway. George could see gray hair and two octopus arms holding the steering wheel—Aunt Octopus.

Honk! Honk!

"Let's go down," George's mother said. "And, George, *please*, remember your manners."

George's mother hurried out of the bedroom and down the stairs.

"Come on, Lucky." George put Lucky down. "She's here."

Honk! Honk!

"Let's go down. And, Lucky, *please*, remember your manners."

Dog Greetings

Honk! Honk!

Lucky raced down the stairs. To Lucky, the sound of a horn meant visitors, and Lucky loved visitors. When people came to visit they always patted him and rubbed him behind the ears. One of his most important jobs was to welcome new people.

Lucky had lived with the boy for almost a year now. He knew what his jobs were.

When the boy threw the rubber newspaper, Lucky was expected to chase it and bring it back to the boy. When he did this the boy said, "Good dog!"

Lucky was expected to clean up any bits of food dropped on the floor when his family was eating. When he did this the woman said, "Good dog!"

He was expected to protect his family. He barked when someone came to the door or when strangers came into the backyard. He kept the squirrels from coming onto the back porch. When he did this the man said, "Good dog!"

He also had learned some things that he was *not* to do.

Roll on dead things.

Make puddles in the house.

Chew on the boy's baseball glove.

When he did these things his people said, "Bad dog!" The rules were clear. The rules made him feel safe.

He ran out of the house into the driveway. A visitor was getting out of a car. Lucky was just in time. Everyone was hugging her.

Lucky bounded down the driveway full speed. He got ready for his typical greeting—

sniffs and licks and pats. He neared the people. He stopped short.

Sniff. Sniff.

There was a new scent in the air.

Sniff. Sniff.

The smell was coming from the front seat
of the visitor's car.

It was an animal smell. The car door was
open. Lucky hurried over for a better look.

Yes, his nose had not failed him. There on
the front seat of the car was an animal.

It did not look like the squirrels Lucky
chased up the oak tree. It did not look like the
tabby cat next door. Or the possum he'd
found on the road last week.

It was a different kind of animal. It was
white with curly hair.

Lucky knew what to do when he ran into
a new animal. It was his job to protect his
people. He had to show right away who was
boss.

He raised the hair on his back and let out
a low growl.

GGRRRRR!

The car animal did not answer.

GGRRRRR! He growled again.

Still no answer.

Lucky's visitor manners were forgotten. He had to protect his people. He guessed the distance. He jumped.

He soared right into the car. Direct hit. He attacked the animal.

He sunk his teeth into the animal's skin and shook his head back and forth. What was it? It was an animal but not an animal. It was something wild and furry.

He dragged it out into the driveway for a better fight. He must protect his people.

The woman screamed. "Auntie's coat!" she said. "Auntie's sheepskin coat!"

GGRRRR!

Lucky shook his head again.

The man grabbed Lucky by the back of the neck and pulled. Lucky would not let himself be pulled away. He sank his teeth deeper into the soft car animal.

"Help!"

The man pulled harder but Lucky would not let go.

The scent of animal was all around him now.

He had smelled some wonderful things in his life. Ham, cheese, a frog squashed on the road, the possum.

But this was different. This was new. This was the most wonderful, wild, irresistible smell he had ever experienced.

He shook his jaws back and forth.

GRRR!

"AAAAAAAAAA!"

Down came a purse on Lucky's head. The man pulled harder. Lucky's jaws came loose.

Lucky didn't feel the pain. He didn't feel the roughness of the man jerking him away. His attention was fixed on the animal. It lay in the driveway, not moving.

He had shown it who was boss. He had done his job.

Lucky wagged his tail and looked up at the

man. He waited to hear the words "Good dog."

But the man looked down at Lucky and pointed his finger and said the other words:

"Bad dog!"

Slimed!

"Lucky!" George yelled. He ran over to Lucky. He patted him to calm him down. It didn't work. George's father held Lucky tightly in his arms.

Lucky fought to get free. He made swimming motions with his feet in the air in the direction of the sheepskin jacket. His eyes rolled with the effort. He barked and squirmed.

"Bad dog!" George's father said again.

"It's okay!" Aunt Octopus said. "It's just an old jacket. I got it at a yard sale."

"It is *not* okay," said George's mother, look-

ing at Lucky. "That dog should know better."

"It really *is* okay."

"Let's go inside."

George's mother led Aunt Octopus toward the house. George watched them walk away. Aunt Octopus had on a red sweatsuit. A picture of Santa Claus was painted on the front. Her gray hair was pulled back in a bun. It was strange to see clothes like that on someone so old.

Aunt Octopus turned and winked at George. He didn't say a word. When his mother called Lucky "that dog" it was time to be quiet.

He turned back to Lucky. Lucky had stopped wiggling. He patted Lucky. Lucky wagged his tail and licked George's hand.

George smiled.

Lucky had saved him! No Octopus hugs this time! In all the excitement Aunt Octopus had forgotten. For once he wouldn't be slimed. No kisses and hugs for him!

But . . . He watched Aunt Octopus walk toward the house. It was not a good beginning. She patted the sheepskin jacket as she walked up the stairs to the porch.

Erf!

When she touched the jacket Lucky lunged forward again.

George had never seen Lucky get so excited.

George's mother frowned back at George. They disappeared into the house.

"What got into Lucky?" said George's father.

George shook his head. "I don't know. Maybe he thinks that jacket is an animal."

"Lucky better behave himself while your aunt is here."

George nodded. "He'll be good. He was just excited about having company."

George's father looked at Lucky. "We'll see how it goes," he said. "But for today let's keep him outside."

"It's Christmas Eve, Dad. Lucky needs to be with us."

"I'm sorry, son. We can't have Lucky acting up with company here."

George took Lucky from his father and held him close.

"You know we all have to be on our best behavior this week," said George's father.

He looked at Lucky. "And that means Lucky, too."

"Be good, Lucky," George said, "or else."

"Just a minute," Aunt Octopus called from the porch. She hurried down the steps. The jacket was gone.

Lucky's fur stood up. In one leap he was on the ground. His nose sniffed the air.

She headed toward George, her arms stretched out wide.

"I didn't even say a proper hello to George. How's my favorite nephew? Now give us a hug!"

Before George could move it happened.

Octopus arms!

"And a big, *big* kiss for my favorite nephew."

SMACK!

George wiped his face with the back of his hand.

Slimed!

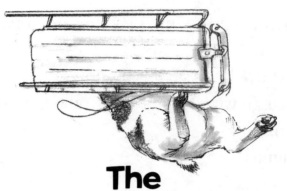

The
Broken Record Bark

She was gone. *It* was gone. The car animal was inside the house.

Lucky ran up the steps and pressed his nose against the crack at the back door and sniffed. He could not even get a whiff of the animal.

"Move, Lucky."

With his foot the boy pushed Lucky off the step. The boy walked up the steps and went into the house. The man walked up the steps and went into the house.

Lucky walked up the steps and . . .

BAM!

The door slammed shut. He was left outside.

He waited. George would let him in. He scratched the door a few times. George did not come.

Being left outside had to do with the words *Bad dog.*

He hated those words. They always meant that something bad was about to happen to him. Like a whack on the behind or being put outside. They meant that a rule had been broken.

Lucky sniffed again at the door. He thought he had obeyed all the rules. He had not bitten or drooled on anyone. He had not allowed the car animal to harm his family. He had greeted the visitor. No! He had *not* greeted the visitor! That must be it. He must greet the visitor.

First, though, he had to figure out how to get into the house.

A bark might work.

Lucky tried to remember his barking lessons. His mother had taught him many different kinds of barks. There was the Chain Letter Bark.

He used that bark at night. When the dog down the street would bark, then Lucky would bark back. Then the dog *across* the street would bark and so on. That would not work now.

There was the Demand Bark. One short bark to show his people what he wanted.

Erf!

He barked at the back door. Now they would open it and let him in.

Erf!

Nobody came. Maybe they hadn't heard him.

He tried it again.

Erf!

Still nothing.

Maybe this situation called for a different bark. The Broken Record Bark. You bark over and over like a broken record.

Erf! Erf! Erf! Erf! Erf! Erf! Erf!

It tortures your people into giving you what

you want. He had used it once to teach the boy that he didn't like his doghouse. He would use it now to get the boy to let him into the house.

Erf! Erf! Erf! Erf! Erf! Erf! Erf!

No George.

Erf! Erf! Erf! Erf! Erf! Erf! Erf!

The door swung open.

"Bad dog!" said the man.

The door swung shut.

Lucky rested his head on his front paws. Those words again. He rolled his eyes up at the door and watched and waited.

Bad dog. The words echoed in his mind. He had heard those terrible words twice today. It was not a good day for Lucky.

Memories

George sat with his parents and his aunt in the living room. Christmas Eve was usually the best day of the year.

The house smelled right. The ham cooking in the oven. The popcorn strings for the tree. The pine branches on the mantel.

Everything looked right. Christmas candles twinkled. The ornaments waited in a red box for the tree.

But it didn't feel right. It was hard to enjoy Christmas Eve with Lucky outside.

Aunt Octopus straightened in her chair.

She picked up a brown grocery bag from beside her feet.

"Are you going to cook something?" George asked in a worried voice.

"Not this year," she said. She opened the grocery bag and pulled out a sack of oranges.

"Come here, George," she said. "I'll show you how we used to make pomanders."

"What's a pomander?"

"Come see."

He moved over and sat on the floor beside his aunt. She pulled out a small jar of cloves and began to push them into the orange.

George took a clove and an orange and tried it.

"This smells good," he said.

"This is what I used to give my mother and my sister, Mary, for Christmas every year. They kept them in bowls around the house to make the rooms smell good."

"Old-timey air freshener," said George.

Everyone laughed. "I remember them in Grandma's house," said George's mother.

"I just love coming here for Christmas," said Aunt Octopus. "It reminds me of Christmases long ago."

"Tell us what it was like," said George's father.

George scooted closer to Aunt Octavia. If he couldn't be with Lucky, at least he could hear a story. He pushed a few more cloves into his orange and listened.

"One year Mary gave me a hat for Christmas. I still remember it. A blue pillbox hat with a tiny veil and a feather on the side."

It sounded silly to George. He looked at the door.

"We both loved that hat. The next year I gave the hat back to her for Christmas. I can still see her face when she opened that box."

"Was she mad?" George couldn't imagine giving anyone a used present.

"No," said Aunt Octopus. "She was glad."

"She liked it?"

"She loved it."

"But it was old."

"It didn't matter to her. She loved it any-way."

George wasn't thinking about Lucky now. He smiled.

"So the next year guess what she gave to me."

"The hat?"

"The hat."

George laughed. "Recycled!" he said.

"We gave each other that same hat for twenty years. Until she died."

Aunt Octopus dabbed her eyes. "I never laughed so hard as I did every Christmas morning when I saw that silly hat."

"Did you have a Christmas tree?" George asked.

"Of course," she said. "And we had a special tree for the whole town. We had it in the church and everyone would come and bring decorations for it. It would be covered with candles and the ornaments would be gifts."

"What kind of gifts?"

"Small things. A pomander." She held up

her orange and smiled. "A handkerchief for a man or a piece of fruit for a child. If you liked a certain girl or fellow you would put a gift on the tree for him."

"Did you ever do that?"

She nodded and smiled. "The maddest I ever got with Mary was over a gift on that Christmas tree."

"The hat?"

"Not the hat. It's another story. I'll tell you sometime."

She put down her orange. It was covered with cloves now.

"Talking about gifts reminds me," she said. "I am making a special surprise for *you* for Christmas and I'm going upstairs right now to finish it."

"You don't need to tidy up or anything, do you?" George held his breath.

"No, your room is perfect."

She walked up the stairs. As she walked into George's bedroom they could hear her say, "Elvis, you hound dog!"

Everyone smiled.

George's father stood up.

"Come on, George," he said. "We've got a job to do, too. It's time to bring in our Christmas tree."

George jumped up and hurried to the back door with his father. He loved decorating the tree.

They had picked it out the night before at the Boy Scout tree sale.

It was tall and even with a single point on the top. The perfect tree. It was out in the garage.

Lucky barked and wagged his tail when he saw them.

"Can Lucky help?" George asked. "Aunt Octavia is in her room. He can't bother her."

"Okay," said George's father. "We'll give him another chance. But he has to be on his best behavior."

"He will be," said George. "He will."

O Christmas Tree

When Lucky had almost given up hope, the door swung open. Out walked the man and the boy.

Lucky jumped up. He wiggled and wagged his tail. The boy picked him up and petted him all over.

He was forgiven. Now he would be good. He would follow the rules.

"Come on, Lucky," the boy called.

The boy and the man walked toward the garage. Lucky followed them. The man pulled up the garage door.

Lucky hurried along beside the boy. If they

were going for a ride he did not want to be left behind.

He ran into the garage. He stopped. He sniffed. A tree was standing in the corner!

Lucky poked his nose into the air. He sniffed the tree. It was a fresh tree with the smells of the forest still on it.

He moved closer.

What was a tree doing inside the garage?

The man picked up one end of the tree. The boy picked up the other. They began to carry it toward the house.

The tree was going inside the house!

Lucky wagged his tail and sniffed the tree again as it went up the stairs. He danced back and forth behind the tree. This was exciting!

They carried the tree into the living room and stopped. Lucky cocked his head and watched.

The man put the tree down. He hammered something onto the bottom of the tree and stood it up. Lucky's family stood back and looked at the tree.

Lucky looked at his family, then back at the tree.

Lucky knew what trees were for!

When he was a puppy he made puddles like this:

He would sniff, circle three times, squat and make a puddle.

When he grew up he made puddles a different way:

He would find a tree, sniff it, circle it three times, then lift up his back leg.

Now as he looked at the tree he was confused. Puddles were not allowed in the house. A tree had been brought into the house. Trees were for puddles. Had the rules changed?

Were puddles now allowed in the house? Was this his own personal indoor tree?

Dog Heaven!

He looked at the tree one more time.

Should he or shouldn't he?

Lucky moved closer to the tree.

He sniffed it.

No one said *Bad dog.*
He circled it three times.
Still no *Bad dog.*
He lifted his back leg.
"Bad dog!"

Silent Night,
Howly Night

ERF! ERF!

George lay in his sleeping bag on the floor of his parents' bedroom. His parents were asleep. He was not. Lucky was barking. Outside. In the doghouse.

It had been the worst Christmas Eve ever. Lucky had been in trouble three times.

He had attacked Aunt Octopus's jacket. Then he had barked at the door. Then the Christmas tree incident.

Now he was banned from the house until Aunt Octopus went home. It wasn't Lucky's fault. Everything changed when company came. It was Aunt Octopus's fault.

ERF! ERF!

George squeezed his eyes shut. He couldn't fall asleep. Lucky was alone out in the dog-house.

Lucky was probably cold. Worst of all, he would wake up George's mother and father and Aunt Octopus.

AAOOOOOOOOO!

He had to do something. He remembered when Lucky was a puppy. Lucky would bark like this in the backyard until George went out and slept with him.

That was in the summer. Now it was too cold for George to sleep in the doghouse. He hoped it wasn't too cold for Lucky.

ERF! ERF!

Christmas should be a happy time. He was not happy.

He tried to think about something else. He thought about his stocking hanging up by the fireplace. He hoped he would get a bike for Christmas. A Mondo Mega bike. He had given his mother three pomanders and a sign he had painted. It said, GOOD FOR FREE HUGS ANYTIME. He smiled. She would love it.

Erf! Erf!

The gift for his father was a ceramic dinosaur he had made at school. Blue glaze. He smiled. His dad would love it.

Erf! Erf!!

He didn't have anything for his aunt. His mother had said they would give her one present from the whole family. It was a certificate for ten dance lessons at a dance studio. She would love it. She wanted to learn the mambo.

Erf! Erf!

And Lucky—Lucky was getting a new chew bone, a rubber squeaky pacifier, and some jerky treats.

George pulled the pillow over his head. He began to hum a Christmas carol.

"Joy to the world . . ." He stopped. He was not joyful.

He tried another one.

"Si-lent night"—*AAOOOOOOO*

"Ho-ly night"—*AAOOOOOOO*

"All is calm"—*AOOOOO*

"All is bright"—*AAOOOOOO*

George couldn't stand it anymore. He crawled out of the sleeping bag and tiptoed out of the room.

As he tiptoed past his bedroom, he heard a snore. Aunt Octopus was asleep in his bed.

He ran downstairs and outside.

The frosty grass stung his feet through his socks. He ran over to Lucky and reached down to undo the chain.

Lucky was shivering.

George picked him up and held him close. Lucky licked George's face. George carried Lucky back to the house.

He put Lucky down. Lucky ran straight to the refrigerator. He curled up in a ball in front of the vent where the warm air blew.

Lucky was not shivering now. Surely it would be okay to leave him here.

"I trust you, Lucky," George whispered. "I know that you won't do anything else bad."

Lucky didn't move or wag his tail. His eyes were closed. He was fast asleep.

George turned and tiptoed back upstairs. Back past Aunt Octopus snoring in his bed. Back to his sleeping bag on the floor of his parents' room.

He heard the steady sounds of their breathing. They had not heard George leave or come back.

In the morning they might be mad because he had let Lucky in. But this would be a way for him to show them that Lucky could behave.

He closed his eyes. He thought once more about Lucky sleeping in front of the refrigerator. He hoped he was right.

Wake-Up Duty

Lucky stretched and opened his eyes. Morning was his favorite time of day.

He loved waking up in front of the refrigerator. He loved the warm air that blew out of the vent and warmed the spot on the floor where he slept.

He loved the feeling of a good stretch. One leg first and then the other.

But most of all he loved wake-up duty. It was his job to wake up the boy.

The woman would usually say:

"Go get George."

And he would run upstairs, jump on the

boy's bed, dig in the covers and lick the boy until his eyes opened. Then they would wrestle on the bed. The boy would laugh and hug him and they would go downstairs for breakfast.

Licks and hugs. Pats and wrestles. Lucky loved wake-up duty.

He got up and stretched, one leg first and then the other. The boy's mother was not awake yet. But it was time.

He ran upstairs into the boy's room. He ran in and stopped.

There was a suitcase on the floor. It was open. He hurried over to get a better look.

Sniff. Sniff. What was inside?

Some clothes.

Sniff. Sniff.

He smelled the clothes. These were the clothes of the visitor. The visitor who had brought the car animal. Maybe the animal was in here!

Wake-up duty was forgotten.

He began to dig in the clothes. He used his best digging motion.

Paw over paw.

Clothes flew in all directions.

Paw over paw.

He had to get to the bottom. He nosed in deeper and deeper . . .

No animal.

He lifted his head and looked around the room.

He saw the bed. The boy. He had almost forgotten Wake-up duty!

He stretched once more for good measure. Then headed for the bed.

With one quick jump he was on the bed.

Erf!

He dug into the mound of covers. Time for hugs and pats. Licks and wrestles.

Erf!

Paw over paw he dug into the bed.

The boy would wake up and hug him and pat him and . . .

"AAAEEEEEEE!"

It was not the boy!

Lucky struggled to get away.

"AEEEEEEE!" the visitor screamed.

Lucky was a brave dog. He was not afraid of the tabby cat next door, or the backyard squirrels, or even Oreo, the doberman up the street.

Up until this moment there had been only one thing in the world that Lucky was afraid of—thunder.

Any time day or night when he heard the rumble of a thunderstorm coming his way he knew what to do.

He would crawl under the sofa. Only there, in the darkness under the sofa, was he safe.

Now he had something new to fear. This visitor. This screaming person. This person who had taken over HIS house, HIS boy's bed.

He twisted in the covers. He could not get off the bed.

"AAEEEEE!"

The boy ran into the room.

"Lucky!" he yelled.

The rest of his family ran in.

"Lucky!" they all yelled.

Lucky twisted free. He didn't stop to hear the words *bad dog*. He ran.

Out the door he went, down the hall, down the steps, past the indoor tree and to the only spot of true safety that he knew in the house—under the sofa.

Mrs. Minnie's Kennel

George raced after his father. Down the stairs to Lucky. "What are you going to do?" he asked.

His father didn't answer.

Zip zip zip

His father's slippers padded down the stairs. George stayed close behind him.

"What are you going to do to Lucky?"

Still no answer.

Zip zip zip.

They walked into the living room. The tree glowed with sparkling ornaments. The stockings bulged. Brightly colored presents waited in piles. George hurried past them. He could only think about Lucky. George knew where he was hiding. Lucky always hid under the sofa.

George's father stopped and looked once at the sofa. Then he walked over to the telephone. He looked at a number on the book beside the phone. He started punching buttons.

"Who are you calling?" George had a bad feeling about the phone.

"Mrs. Minnie."

"The kennel?"

"Yes. Mrs. Minnie's Kennel."

"Please Dad! Don't do it!"

He didn't stop dialing.

"George, we have to do it. We can't have Lucky and your aunt in the same house. Lucky will have to go away until after Christmas."

He punched the last few numbers and listened.

George blinked back his tears.

George thought about Lucky being all alone. He thought about Lucky being alone for Christmas.

Lucky's presents were all wrapped under the tree. His new chew bone, his squeaky doggy pacifier, his jerky treats. He would not be here to open them.

Lucky's stocking was hanging by the fireplace next to George's. He would not be here to see what Santa brought him.

He thought about how much Lucky would love Christmas carols. He would point his nose into the air and sing with them. *Aaaoooooo!* He would not be singing any carols at Mrs. Minnie's Kennel.

He had to be home for Christmas.

"You can't, Dad!"

"I can."

George could not hold the tears back now.

"Please, Dad. One more chance."

His father shook his head.

"Why can't Aunt Octopus go home instead?" George said. "She's the one causing the problem, not Lucky!"

George was yelling now. "Lucky behaved himself just fine before she came!"

"Now, George. Calm down."

"I hate her! She's just an old octopus and I hate her!"

"George!"

George looked at his father.

He hung up the phone. He was looking past George. He had a funny look on his face. George turned and followed his gaze.

Aunt Octopus was in the doorway. George's mother was next to her.

Aunt Octopus looked like someone had just knocked the wind out of her.

Her mouth was in a big O. Her eyes had a hurt look.

George's mother stared at George with her most disappointed look.

Nobody said a word.

George wished he could crawl under the sofa with Lucky.

Under the Sofa

Lucky huddled in the darkness under the sofa. He crouched low at the back in the middle. In the middle was a spot where no hands could possibly reach him.

He had learned this position when he was a puppy. He had chewed the man's briefcase. He had only chewed a little on the corner. But the man had been upset.

Lucky crouched lower and listened.

The man and the boy were talking in loud voices.

Maybe he would hear some words that he

knew. Some words that would explain this terrible time.

Lucky knew a lot of words. He had learned the people's language as a puppy.

He had learned the good words first—*dinner, car, walk, treat, ham,* and the best words, *GOOD DOG.* He hadn't heard any good words lately.

He had also learned some bad words—*vacuum, doghouse, vet, rabies shot, flea dip, kennel,* and the worst words, *bad dog.* He had heard those words too many times.

When he had tried to defend his family from the car animal.

When he had tried to get them to open the door and let him in.

And then there was the tree problem.

Lucky closed his eyes and tried not to think about it.

There was another word, *Christmas.* He had heard that word a lot lately. He wondered what it meant. It had something to do with all the strange things that were happening.

So far *Christmas* had only meant getting into trouble. Lucky decided that *Christmas* must be a bad word.

His heart beat faster. He kept his eyes closed.

What had happened? The morning had started out like any other morning. He had gone to wake up the boy and. . . . He didn't want to think about it.

The last two days had been too confusing.

The boy was not in his room anymore.

Lucky could not do anything right. It was worse than when he was a puppy.

He listened to the boy and the man. He heard some other words that he knew. Bad words, the worst words. He crouched even lower. He made himself into a tight ball.

The words were *Mrs. Minnie's Kennel.*

More Memories

George sat on his parents' bed and stared at the wall. Christmas was ruined. He had ruined it.

He kept thinking about the way Aunt Octavia's face had looked when he had said that he hated her.

He didn't hate her exactly. He liked her. He had just been mad at her. Now he had ruined everything.

George brushed away a tear.

There was a knock on the door. He didn't answer. Aunt Octavia walked in.

George's throat was tight. He couldn't say anything.

"I never finished my story," she said. "About my sister."

George couldn't look at her face.

"The maddest that I ever got with her was over the Christmas tree gifts."

She sat down on the bed next to him.

"Well, there was a certain fella that we both liked. John Dadismon. He was a fine, handsome young man. The preacher's son."

George peeked up at her.

"I embroidered a handkerchief for him one Christmas. You should have seen it. Flowers and vines and his initials on the corner. I wrapped it up and wrote on the outside: 'To John, From Octavia.' I hung it on the tree at church."

She stopped for a second.

"Well, when I went outside to see if John was coming, my sister took that present from the tree. And where it said 'From Octavia' she changed it to say 'From Mary.'"

She laughed.

"John opened that present and walked up to Mary and kissed her on the hand."

"He did?"

"He did. Mary was like that. Always up to something."

"What did you do?"

"We had our biggest fight ever. Right there in the church. All over that silly gift. You wouldn't believe the things we said to each other."

"What happened?"

"While we were arguing John left with Abigail Crump."

Aunt Octopus laughed.

"You were pretty mad at your sister?"

"Very mad. For that one moment, I actually hated my own sister. Can you imagine that?"

"I can," said George. "What happened?"

"Oh, I forgave her later. I could never stay mad at Mary."

"I guess there are some things that you can't forgive," said George, "like what I said downstairs."

Aunt Octavia thought for a moment.

"Do you love Lucky?" she asked.

"Of course."

"Have you ever been mad at him?"

George remembered one time in a parking lot. Lucky would not walk on his leash. He had rolled over and made George pull him. A crowd of people had clapped and cheered for Lucky.

He remembered another time. He had left Lucky alone in the station wagon for just a moment. When he got back Lucky had torn up the grocery bags and scattered the groceries everywhere.

He remembered one other time. It had been during a baseball game. Lucky had stolen the ball and had started a game of Keep-Away on the ball field.

Yes, he had been pretty mad at Lucky.

He nodded at Aunt Octavia. "Lots of times," he said.

"Did you forgive him?"

"Of course," said George. "I could never stay mad at Lucky!"

"That's the way I feel about you," said Aunt Octavia. "And I'm not mad at Lucky, either. He's just being a dog."

She wrapped her arms around George and hugged him. He hugged her back and for once he did not think of octopus arms. He smelled her cinnamon smell. Her arms were warm and soft.

"Let's start over," said Aunt Octavia. "Let's go downstairs and open the presents and have Christmas."

She stood up. George didn't get up.

"What's wrong now?" she asked.

"Lucky," said George. "Dad wants to send him to the kennel. How can we have Christmas without Lucky?"

"Hmm," she sat back down. "I think your father might change his mind about the kennel," she said. "But we still need a way to get Lucky out from under the sofa."

George nodded.

"Maybe he would come out for a dog treat."

George shook his head.

"A piece of ham?"

George shook his head again. He thought and thought. What would make Lucky come out?

"I have an idea," Aunt Octavia said. "I think it's time for me to give Lucky his Christmas present."

Dog Presents

Lucky waited deep under the sofa. It was quiet now. The people were gone. Even so, he would not come out. He had learned something about hiding from watching the tabby cat next door.

She would wait for hours at a chipmunk hole. Patiently and quietly she would wait. And then, when the chipmunk finally came out, POUNCE! She always caught it.

Lucky was not taking any chances. Nothing would get him out from under this sofa.

He heard footsteps. He heard the man's voice first.

"Come on, Lucky."

Lucky sniffed the air.

Sniff sniff.

Dog biscuits.

He would never come out for a dog biscuit.

He waited. More footsteps.

"Come on out, Lucky."

This time it was the boy's mother.

Sniff sniff.

HAM! His mouth watered.

No. He would not come out. Not even for *HAM.*

He waited. More footsteps.

This time it was the boy and the visitor. He must *not* come out!

Sniff sniff.

He pushed his nose forward and sniffed the air. Could it be?

Sniff sniff.

It must be!

Sniff sniff.

Yes it was!

The car animal! It was on the floor in front of the sofa!

He dug his nails into the rug. He must not come out.

But he could not resist the smell. He inched forward. Inch by inch. Sniffing and crawling. Sniffing and crawling and . . .

He scrambled out from under the sofa.
POUNCE!

The boy grabbed him. He was caught! The boy hugged him. He put him back down on the floor in front of a paper hump. A big crinkly hump that smelled like the car animal!

Lucky knew about presents. Presents were a game where people hid something in paper and he tore off the paper to find out what it was.

The big present sat in front of him. The irresistible smell told him exactly what it was.

The car animal.

He pounced. He ripped the paper. The

pieces of red and green paper came off in long shreds. He ripped and tore the paper until none was left. He looked at the soft white animal.

It was puffy now like a pillow.

Lucky lunged forward and sank his teeth into it. He shook his head back and forth.

He rolled on it a few times. It was soft and smelled wonderful.

He looked up at the boy and the visitor and the man and the woman.

No one said, "Bad dog."

"Merry Christmas, Lucky," the visitor said.

It was for him!

Dog Heaven.

Recycled!

George watched Lucky roll on the pillow. It was Aunt Octopus's surprise. She had made a pillow for Lucky out of her old sheepskin jacket.

Everything was perfect. The Mondo Mega bike gleamed beside the Christmas tree. His mother loved her sign. She had already used it for fifteen hugs. His father liked his dinosaur. He was going to put it on his desk for a paperweight. Aunt Octavia had been so excited about her dance lessons that she did dance steps all around the Christmas tree.

He looked at the tree and all the unwrapped presents. Everything was *almost* perfect. If only he had a present for Aunt Octavia. The dance lessons were really from his parents. He wished that he had bought her a blue hat like in the story. It was too late. The stores were closed. Suddenly George had an idea. "I'll be right back," he said.

He ran upstairs and in less than a minute returned with a large rectangular present.

He handed it to Aunt Octavia.

"What can this be?" she asked.

She held it. She felt it. She shook it.

Slowly she pulled down the red wrapping paper.

"Oh," she said.

George held his breath.

"You shouldn't have." She dabbed her eyes. "Elvis, you hound dog!"

Elvis Presley on black velvet.

"Recycled!" said George.

"My favorite kind of gift," she said. "It will always remind me of you and my very best Christmas."

She gave George a big octopus hug.

Joyful Noises

Lucky was lying on his new animal pillow, chewing his new rawhide bone. His back legs pointed straight into the air. The smell of the pillow was all around him. His presents were beside him. His family loved him again.

Dog Heaven!

His people sat around the indoor tree. The boy began to sing. Lucky sat straight up on the pillow and watched. He loved singing.

"Joy to the world, the Lord is come!" The man joined in. Then the boy's mother. Then the visitor.

The visitor! He had never greeted the visi-

tor. Should he do it now? Why not? Lucky ran to the visitor. She opened her arms and with one jump he was in them. He gave her a big lick. Then another. She liked it. She held him tight.

The singing rang around him.

"And heaven and nature sing! And heaven and nature sing!"

It was a happy sound.

Lucky cocked his head once. He knew what to do. He pointed his nose in the air and added his most joyful noise.

AAOOOOO!

Christmas was a good word after all!